Celebration

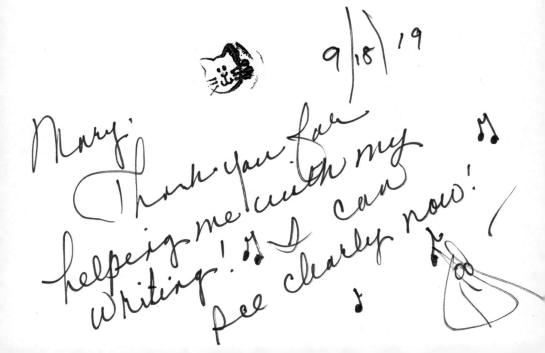

Mary,
Thank you for
helping me with my
writing! ♪♫ I can
see clearly now! ♪

Celebration

Anniecat Chronicles II

Joan Rust

Rev. date: 06/07/2018

To order additional copies of this book, contact:
Xlibris
1-888-795-4274
www.Xlibris.com
Orders@Xlibris.com
780434

KIDS and KINFOLK

I'll love you forever,
I'll like you for always,
As long as I'm living,
My baby you'll be.

Robert Munsch

WAVING

There is a large window over the kitchen sink in the cabin at Bay Mills. The bottom half lifts out of the wall and is set aside; the top half is raised to ceiling hooks. The result is a large, screened view of all the activities along the breakwater and out onto the bay. A beautiful waterwind breezes through the opening, slamming the back door and knocking loose items from atop the cupboards. This kitchen window was a perfect frame for the portrait of my mother as she stood at the sink, preparing a meal or washing up a few dishes. Keeping an eye on all of us, she would look up and wave. Leaving from the cabin or from the house on Hursley Avenue, the last happy memory of our visit was that wave from Mom as she stood on the porch, no matter the time or the weather, to send us off with love. My heart learned a few things watching her. I want those last few minutes with my family and friends, so I am on the porch to wave them down the driveway and on their way ... always.

Air travel has changed our welcomes and goodbyes. TSA more or less greets our loved ones and shuffles them away these days while we stand on the other side of partitions. "Drop and dash" is a heartbreaking new trend ... like cell phones at a family dinner. Families can pull up to the terminal, and with the motor running, watch their children disappear through sliding doors, hauling exactly 50 lbs. of luggage and Mom's cookies already crumbling in the carryon. Some of us manage a staged cheerfulness through this; but, yielding to the tears just past the long term parking lot, turn to give that wave anyway. Seeing my loved ones off is difficult; however, they go back to the lives they have created for themselves which make me proud of them. Also, I know there will be arrivals as well when I welcome a child home at a gate, on the porch, from the window, waving.

TWO BIRTHDAYS

April 10, 1956. 11:00 a.m. Sault Ste. Marie, Michigan. The Rust household on Hursley Avenue. Elva Rust is preparing a cake for her youngest daughter's birthday. The oldest Rust daughter has been staying with her parents while her husband is on maneuvers with the army; and she enters the kitchen to announce that she is about to deliver the first grandchild. The story is that Elva Rust calmly lifted the beater from the cake batter, and without turning it off, set it on the countertop. The birthday child comes home from grade school for lunch and suffers an upset tummy from the excitement of pending birth and/or seeing the kitchen walls covered with her birthday cake. Eddie Rust is called home to transport his first-born to the hospital; and in the anxiety and excitement of the event, suffered an epic nosebleed, so could not linger at War Memorial Hospital Admissions. Leaving one daughter safely at the hospital, he returned home to see to another, care for his nose and help his wife wipe down the kitchen. Tom Beggs was born later that afternoon, a grandson for the Rusts and a special birthday gift for his Aunt Sandy.

BEAUTIFUL SURPRISES

Dear Ryan and Emily: Well, we are still reeling from the happy news!!! Seems such a short time ago I woke up one morning and realized Tommy was with me. I was a long way from home near a proving ground in the Arizona desert and alone. Tom's Dad had to ship out with his company headed across the country to Georgia. But the joy that comes with that first realization of your child is overwhelming, even under less than ideal conditions. Tom has brought me that same joy for 57 years. Jeff was not acquired at a yard sale as Kim keeps telling him, but arrived 14 months after Tom; followed by Kim and then Scott just a little more than a year after her. So you might say each one was "unplanned". You should say, however, like wonderful gifts, they were Beautiful Surprises.

MOMENTUM

This morning Sawyer crept onto the pc screen and began to scoot across the carpet in his beginner crawl toward a red bowl. It is the day in a child's life we all anticipate, but know that his care has been upped a notch (at 6 mos) even as we enjoy these first creeping movements forward. At the same time, in another frame, Lance climbed onto a small tricycle, and by instinct gripped the handlebars and put his little feet on the pedals, road-ready ... or for now (2 yrs) dreaming of racing down the sidewalk. That morning Henrik (3 yrs) began hockey practice. He will pack up his small skates and hit the ice for drills, disappointed, perhaps, that no sticks are allowed yet. Three beloved greatgrandsons who in their forward momentum, keep their GG looking ahead. Meanwhile, the fourth, dear Axel Jeffrey, in the next image, does his thing at 4 weeks. He smiles with his whole sweet face as he poops.

STELLAR

Some years ago, my neighbor's Chesapeake, Breeze, departed our woods and shoreline. She had a retriever's fondness for the most challenging wild places in the brush, and was drawn to water. I followed her through thickets into beaver ponds and unexpected pools of bog at the end of her leash. Set free in her element, she could swim endlessly in the surf off Squaw Point. Breeze the Beast was my guest when her family traveled. In the house she preferred sleeping ON my bed facing the tv, indulging her strange fascination with Dave Letterman. Like most of her breed, she could be reserved, rendering her total friendship significant. The Blau family invited me to stop by and visit their Chesapeake pup the other day. She would be different from Breeze, they advised. Whereas my old friend was a rich brown, this little girl would have a yellow or "dead grass" coat ... and a cautious attitude. She came quietly into the hallway and looked at me with Breeze's golden eyes. I sat down, and Stellar Performance climbed into my lap and laid her head on my heart.

BOOKS AND MUSIC

Dearest. I am sending you Baby Einstein music recordings. These are supposedly good for your brain. Your parents, my grandchildren, were strapped into my car's back seat and I drove around making them listen to scratchy old cd's of the Vienna Philharmonic. Their brains are exemplary, I'm happy to say, but having heard enough of the classics, they now prefer rock or worse. For now, I hope you will give Einstein a chance. Love you forever.

Three year old Henrik is coming to visit GG today. This is an occasion for both of us because he lives in MN and our time together is precious. I wish the weather would cooperate, but it looks as if we will have to be indoors, saving our beach exploration (and real bear hunting with Papa Jeff) for another time. I have his Aunt Molly's giant box of crayons on the table, together with the ancient coloring books and puzzles collected by two generations. He is below the age limit for the old favorites such as Uno and Sorry or Jakob's favorite Chinese Checkers. He is especially unready for the ladder to the loft. Perhaps he may want to just sit with me in the old rocker and hear me read the stories his grandfather loved.

TOMATO PICKLE

Eyes stinging and nose running, Nanny Sawyers peeled and sliced the basket of large, vigorous onions pulled from Pickford soil, pausing to lift a corner of her ever-present apron to her face. I now appreciate that bushel of tomatoes dropped into boiling water one measure at a time to simmer just until the skins began to split. The hands-on work continues as a speared tomato is quickly peeled, then the next and the next, fingers eventually feeling as scalded as the fruit when the chopping begins. Whole bunches of sliced celery were last to leave the sinktop, joining the sugar, vinegar and spices in the big farm kettle of tomatoes and onions waiting on the stove. The recipe would cook down for hours …enough time to sterilize the canning jars. My Grandfather, Ephriam Sawyers, loved this tomato pickle and always had it on his plate, especially with mashed potatoes. Part of today's preserves will come to the table at a special family gathering. What better way to bring my grandparents to the celebration than to taste a memory? My house is filled with familiar, spicy comfort as a small rendition of Nanny's farm kettle bubbles away. With itchy eyes and tender fingers, I think of her, Susan Elizabeth McKee Sawyers, with the familiar affection. There are no shortcuts to becoming a loving grandmother... or to making her tomato pickle.

CANDID MOM

Thank you dear daughter Kim for the candid moment. This is pretty much my real profile as the matriarch... Hard to snap one of those glamorous portraits when I always have a paintbrush, rake or can of WD40 in one hand. You will recognize my favorite shirt from the Moshers' rummage sale — fashionably tied at the waist to keep the tails out of my paint can or the power sprayer. The knot is also a good defense against ticks, as are the socks pulled over the pants cuffs. Please note the coordinated hockey stockings/shirt, nice contrasts to the paddle pants left over from my kayak wardrobe. Am sorry my beloved hat had blown into the woods earlier. Nesting birds are probably already pulling at its tattered straw. On the same day this photo was taken, the mail carrier delivered the new Talbots catalog, a reminder of how far you can fall from high fashion.

TRIBUTE

Sorry we missed "puppy day" Mr. Muggins. I know you are sitting there thinking of Jeff and Laurie with that interloper Labrador cousin in Virginia. You saw the suitcases. Call if you need me — you know how — just bite on speed dial. Verizon was understanding about the last time you used my phone.

Originally bred for a cruel sport called bull-baiting, the English bulldogs have evolved to the lovable tough guys of dogdom. They are the darlings of pet food commercials, the Marine Corps and countless sports teams, and are a boon to professional cleaning companies. Anyone can see this breed's beauty is definitely in the eye of the beholding breeders and owners of bulldogs. But to the family who has the patience to wait as their bulldog makes all decisions, he is a most affectionate, maddeningly clever and loyal friend. It's all a game of wits with the bulldog. Jeff and Laurie's Mr. Muggins walks into a room, sits down and then surveys every surface determining if anything is out of place since he was last there. I've seen cats do this, but the bulldog has his own method of surveillance. If something is not to his liking, he will sit motionless as if turned to stone until you figure out what is bothering him. If you are too slow with this, there is the little bulldog noise... part chitter like a squirrel and part rumbly growl ... and then finally the BIG BARK. Bulldogs are not barkers, but when they decide to make noise, everyone pays attention. The first time I fed Muggs he cleaned his dish, then stood frozen, waiting for my brain to catch up with his. Finally I saw one, stray and unreachable kernel of kibble behind his dish. That he would leave this small gap in the orderliness of his environment was more his concern, I believe, than an escaped tasty morsel. Bulldogs require regular exercise. They try to argue this by appearing comatose when you bring out the leash or, if you get him as far as the sidewalk, by sitting and refusing to move. Sometimes Muggs will start off well, trotting at a brisk pace showing that distinctive bulldog swagger (dog of enormous confidence!). When you reach a good distance 4 or 5 blocks from home, he will sit down and refuse to go further. After a reasonable wait, during which it usually begins to rain or the sun goes down, I find just dragging him home the only thing to do. This is strenuous, and can be embarrassing depending on the amount of traffic passing us. He is working on this little problem in obedience class, along with throwing himself to the floor when told to lie down and his inappropriate affection toward every other dog in the class, including the males. He, like all bulldogs, has a noticeable issue with gas, only partly solved by a daily spoonful of yogurt; and he snores heartily the second his eyes close. His chin has to be wiped, and his squished up little nose needs to be lotioned. He loves to be bathed and dried with the hair dryer, but needs conditioner for his skin and oil for the pads of his feet. He is a project. Bulldogs have no tail to wag, but swing their entire body in a joyous rhumba when they see you. They do not jump up on you like normal dogs because their stumpy legs do not allow this. They merely assume a position in front of you and a stare, a chitter-growl to make sure you notice.... and wait. They always end up on the sofa next to you because you have lifted them or in the bed beside you because you have pushed them up there. And just before he starts to snore, he'll produce one last fart and give you that bulldog love look. I am smitten.

SCHOOL BELL CRAFTS

Auntie Carol's store has become one of our happy memories. School Bell Crafts opened in 1991, shortly after Auntie retired from teaching. She and Uncle Ken went into town one day for groceries and came home with a log cabin. Soon after, the cabin door was open from Memorial Weekend to Labor Day, for 24 years, at a site on their "other place" property in the heart of Stonington. Carol opened her business to market the quilts she created, but ultimately it provided an outlet for artists and crafters across the peninsula. We had nearly a week to be a little sad about Auntie's second retirement before we heard her next plan. Always appreciative of local creativity, she is organizing the First Annual Stonington Arts and Crafts Fair to be held just down the road this July. In addition to local crafts, she plans for food, music, raffles, bake sales and good weather. Auntie Carol, on a roll. Again.

FAST PUPPY

For Ryan Beggs and his sons, Sawyer Daniel and Beau Charles. *Oh, the excitement and anxiety of the Puppy's hockey games where I have to run back and forth to the concession stand, consuming gallons of watery hot chocolate to help me deal with my rink rage! Ryan scored a goal for the high school team (the Eskymos) last night, his senior year on the ice. Fortunately, I was not off foraging, and have the moment sealed in my memory and my heart. I began calling him "Fast Puppy" about the time he put on that pair of used Tacks we found at "Play It Again Sports" in Marquette... and then skated onto ice. He had been tearing up the sidewalks and inline venues for years, wearing down wheels in one exultant stage of happy momentum. He was a late starter in hockey. At one of his earliest practices, I watched a team of young boys lined up for a drill, standing on the ice waiting for their turn. Ryan was in line, sorta, but skating in little arcs, stick to the ice, back and forth as if headed for an imagined goal, constantly moving. Everyone should have something in their life which fills them with self-realization and pure excitement. I believe that is what Ryan feels when he plays hockey... hurtling into his element on seamless ice and joy.* What fun it will be to watch the three of them on skates. Go Puppies!!!

FRUITCAKE

The post said "... made this on Christmas Eve..." How can anyone make a good fruitcake as late as day before Christmas??? Gramma the Great Elva started her fruitcakes shortly after we had eaten the last of Aunt Reta's suet pudding on Thanksgiving. The Great's cakes were wrapped in cheesecloth and regularly soaked in brandy Grampa Ed had smuggled in from Canada. She tried several clever hiding places in the basement to keep Grampa away from the cakes, none of which were safe from his nose for such treasure ... and his desire to outwit Gramma the Great.

FRAGRANCES

My house is filled with such beautiful sunshine this morning and the most excellent fragrances! During the weekend Laurie pampered us all with her new proficiency in massage therapy using healing oils. Her recent certification is bringing blissful relief to aching muscles and stressed spirit. The scent of the oils is mystical. We were also treated to her addictive caramelized onion spread cooked on my stovetop, the maddeningly wonderful fragrance of sweet onions and garlic simmering in butter blending with a mist of orange from a diffuser. Tom, Jeff, the bulldog and I were so transported by this aroma therapy, we hardly noticed the Packers losing a game in another universe.

TIGHTIE WHITIES

Before 5 a.m. today, Scott, Don and I were at the edge of Michigan's longest deer runway awaiting their plane to Detroit-Ft. Lauderdale. Watching their luggage disappear at check-in was an act of faith. They had arrived from Florida last week, their bags taking a separate journey and showing up in a cab two days later. Thus, they began their vacation in hurried purchases of WalMart underwear and toiletries. I am thinking of that afternoon when we laughed at the results of their shopping trip spread out over the room: "tightie whities" and sale bin t-shirts, 50 cent flip-flops and miniature size toothpaste and deodorants! I'm holding onto that funny scene to cheer me this morning as their plane takes them farther South with each word I type.

UNCLE CLIVE

Uncle Clive Sawyers, owned two pair of magnificent draft horses. I recall two had rather racy names: Toots and Dolly. When he retired from the large farm near Pickford, he found a way to keep those horses... bring them to Mackinac Island for summer jobs. So, each year he, Aunt Sara and the two teams spent their summers fashionably on the island. One morning, back at the farm, he went out to the barn to see to the horses, and his life ended in the fresh straw of their stall. The story is Aunt Sara found him there, gone suddenly from the heart attack, the horses standing absolutely still beside him in respect and grief.

EMPTY NEST

As soon as my little girl was on the plane, I walked down to baggage claim and had a good cry before heading home for a nap. Empty Nest Syndrome is a recurring ailment, beginning when children reach school age and are out of sight for long hours. Painful bouts with ENS are experienced each time you see your child drive away, fly off, or just turn a corner in life. I know their lives are full, but each child leaves its own special spot in the nest empty. The best cure is to start on the towels and sheets, freeze the leftovers and begin planning for the next time you are together.

SENDOFF

This is the 48th year since the last first day of school for my children, but I remember those sendoffs. I always tried to stir up a little excitement about the future, and attempted to reinforce an awareness of the potential in each of them with small pep talks as they hurried out the door. I am able to recall some of the "first day" outfits. Earlier years: new from heads to toes, in outfits selected by their mother who wished the world to see them as promising and as darling as she saw them; Later years: just one degree off passably scruffy, their protective cover used to ensure blending into the masses. It was the 60's. Designers were content then to put their labels on *haute couture*, never dreaming they could someday dress children for school in t-shirts, jeans or gym shorts emblazoned with their logos. However, the words that followed my children out the door remain the same … "do your best."

FIRESIDE

A fire is burning in the woodstove. Jeff has left me a comfortable supply of firewood, and it will find its way through the back door, ensuring another winter of cozy, firelit hours. Like today, he and Laurie will be with me to savor this comfort. Scott is here for a winter visit, and Kim is home to stay. Her dog, Peace, now shares the fireside with the bulldog. Tom has stopped by to check the ceiling fan and to enjoy this day with "the wild bunch." Later, after a favorite family meal (a pasta pyramid), these grown children will stretch out on the floor close to the fire... warm, safe, loved.

THE GREATGRANDCHILDREN

May, 2018. In Hancock, Jakob puts his skates in the closet and heads for the ball field, only days before graduation. Somewhere in Pennsylvania, Sawyer and Beau unpack their sticks and new Penguin shirts, while Henrik tries his hockey moves warming up at soccer practice in Minnesota. His little brother Axel holds a book and watches out the window for Papa Jeff. Lance Wm. runs along a North Carolina beach on the most amazing long legs and joy ever gifted to a young boy as Skylar Jo watches from her mother's arms. The first little greatgranddaughter smiles and smoothes a pink ruffle away from her view of the ball … there … waiting for "someday".

YOOPER

(Resident of Michigan's Upper Peninsula)

Home is where the heart is.

Pliny the Elder

HOME

Without written release by the U.S. Surgeon General, waiving formal review and approval of Medicare and Blue Cross, before the boys could question it, I claimed my car from daughter Kim's garage yesterday and drove home to Stonington. I did circle the block once to show off my driving skills for her, then turned to Maverick FM and hit the open road. I walked through the door of my cottage to the familiar scent of the cedar walls, once again comforted and grateful the distinctive fragrance of home never changed over the years, despite the recurring aromas from pots and roasters of my family's favorite meals. There is a certain light in these rooms reflected from the Bay which is uplifting even on stormy days, enhanced by a cozy fire in season. I've been told my house is home to Angels of Abundance. I believe this, and am thankful for them. Today I am surrounded by their benevolence, happy to be home and healing, thinking of the angels in my family who cared for me and made it possible for me to be back here. Here's to the familiar, the consoling peacefulness... and to new wellness, its optimism and excitement, as well as unlimited potato chips and chocolate milk.

REWARDS

My yard work continues, and I return wheelbarrows filled with leaves and twigs to the woods daily. The rewards of this simple labor are budding hydrangea and viburnum freed from a winter cover, ovals of dependable daylily and hosta shoots, and the backbone of my gardening success ... ancient iris and peony already growing through their blanket of tattered leaves. As most complain about yard work, I continue to find it uplifting seeing the evidence of one season looking after the next as it departs. As I have written to my friends and children, these days of tidying things up are a small tradeoff for the beauty of my trees. I thank God that I have these days of discovery and amazement in my 84th spring, and that my health and the old wheelbarrow are still up to such joyful labor.

HOT FLASHES

The first warm weather report in seven months moved BFF Darlene and me to hit the road. We fired up the Mighty Honda and sped North on clear pavement, heady with thoughts of shopping 30% off, bootless, clad in light jackets. Much to our delight, the temperature was 79 degrees when we reached Marquette. The warm weather held through the day, but the real heat wave traveled home with us inside the car. Sometime during the winter, its AC system had expired, unnoticed. With windows down, stripped as far down as decent ladies of our age are allowed, Darlene and I returned home, windblown, shouting post-shopping chitchat to each other. Mighty Honda went into Jerry's Service this morning. Jim and Bruce have kept my vintage car on the road for these 13 years; and they were sympathetic but professional about my complaint. We agreed they would restore the air conditioning but there wasn't anything they could do about hot flashes.

BEAR STORY

The first warning was phoned to me by the Neighbors Lachat. Another overcast, clammy day was predicted along the shoreline of Squaw Point. Dispirited gardeners and 4th of July planners faced further setback in their efforts to create summer landscapes. My burn pile of seasonal debris remained sodden atop last year's Christmas tree. Fragile plants waited just inside the garage door, losing hope. Only the mosquitoes thrived, turning us into inspired sprinters as we dashed from door to door pursued by hellish swarms. Damp, dismal and dripping insect repellant, we waited for June to occur. Instead, a bear happened.

Here on Stonington, bears share the turf with us; and, as in any community, some residents are less polite than others. It is widely believed that bears are happy to stay away from us. In Alaska we were told to tie bells or tin cups on our packs so that we made enough noise to alert the bears; thus reminding them of being happier away from us. I belong to the narrow-minded believers who consider bears, at their best, impolite.

We experience the occasional bears on this Point, passing through on their way to and from the campground. They plunder the bird feeders, knock over the grills, drive the dogs crazy, then move on down the peninsula. But, I am the fearful lady who imagines the next one will be the bear with bad genes, and am cautious. This one bent the Gendron's feeder poles to the ground 400 feet from my front door. A few more yards down the road, he easily carried off Lachat's feeder as well as their garbage (and the large container holding it). Reports confirm seeing and hearing him. Not a shy one, this bear. Until he wanders off on his own or with the DNR's help, I have discontinued the Endless Buffet my birds, squirrels and chipmunks have rated 5 stars. Sadly, I have also given up al fresco Snickers bars on the way to the mailbox. Don't want my last words to be: "I was right about bears!"

HEAT WAVE

Hot and humid at Stonington. This opens an unexplored conversation for us Yoopers. Everyone recounts the last time (usually a couple of years ago) they turned on an AC, documenting for you the hours they have been running on "Arctic" mode during the past week. This has caused the Alger-Delta Electric stock to soar. Hordes of field mice, hairy spiders and red squirrels, evicted from dormant outdoor compressors, now roam the area. Jeff installed an AC unit in my home two years ago, and it has been my social salvation more than once. Thirteen (unsuperstitious) Bunco ladies showed up Tuesday evening; Wednesday, the bridge group enjoyed soothing breezes in my humble cottage; and Thursday I served roasted and basted big ass ham with creamed new potatoes and fresh cooked green beans to a dinner table as we diners sipped chilled wine and discussed the weather. Yesterday the wind switched from the west to somewhat northerly and blew the humidity away from Stonington, lowering the temperature to a beautiful Yooper comfort range. A couple of homeless bats are already circling my compressor.

FLU SHOT

Have you had your flu shot? A good opener for conversation this time of year. We can then move on to disclosing our favored vaccine suppliers. The market being what it is, we can choose from any number of businesses offering the convenience of a clinic while checking out sale merchandise. Perhaps we will hear Starbucks has come out with Pumpkin Latte vaccine (grandes for Blue Cross customers). Our family doctors are ever vigilant, greeting patients with "Have you had your flu shot" as they open the door to the examining room. My personal choice is Walgreens because I like the idea of my immunization paying forward for some person who has slipped through the system. This brought me to their pharmacy counter this Halloween Eve and then to one of two chairs off to the side of lines of customers who appeared to have shown up for some sort of prescription social hour. (PROBABLY DIDN'T HAVE THEIR FLU SHOT!) A nice gentlemen in his work clothes took the other chair and we began some sort of vigil while the world searched for a cure for cancer, babies were born, and then we began to have a conversation. As people trouped by us coughing and sneezing, he ventured a guess that we were going to get the flu before we had our flu shot. He said that he, too, was puzzled by the questionnaire giving three choices to answer the question: "Are you presently sick?" (Yes) (No) (I don't know). We felt the pregnancy statement didn't apply to either of us. After 47 minutes, I said I worried that my boys would hear I was hanging out with some guy in Walgreens. "How big are your boys?" "How big is your wife?" When we finally made it behind the screen to the grand event, we smoothed down our little red bandaids, wished each other a Happy Halloween, and agreed the romance was over. Sadly, we didn't exchange names or addresses. We could have sent a card every year wishing each other a happy and healthy flu season.

STORAGE

Perhaps ducks are more clever than I thought. Free spirited flocks of mallards frolic daily along my shoreline. Their numbers and actions appear to celebrate Fall Break ... one big party in the waters a short waddle from my front deck. I have withheld this news from my son for days. The higher water level this year has submerged Jeff's hunting site; and the portable blind, a happy setting for him and his hunting partners, remains in pieces at the back of my garage. The ducks are left to party on through this season. Big Brother Tommy arrives from Dollar Bay tonight towing his boat. A summer of boating will end at the garage behind his cabin here, storing until spring those happy memories of sunshine days on the waters off Keweenaw. Thinking of something to cheer my boys today, I have come up with Mom's Monster Meatloaf and a pumpkin cheesecake, served away from the sight of duck celebration and open water.

DICHOTOMY

Winter is imminent when I put a runner on the deck. Each year the sturdy strip of carpet comes out of a corner in the garage to make its announcement that snow and ice are on the way. With a borrowed stapler, I will fasten the runner along the lines of punctures from previous years, making certain its edges won't be lifted by weeks of shoveling. Somehow, each fall the old carpet manages to look fresh ... and reassuring. It keeps us from sliding off the deck and into physical therapy. Today there will be a mixed message just outside the door. The geraniums still blooming profusely and bravely in their pots, sitting on the first sign of winter.

COWGIRL

My parents raised a healthy child by telling her cowboys ate a diet of fresh vegetables. These, I believed, came from the Soo Coop produce section and, later, from misted bins at Elmer's Market. At times my hearty appetite for vegetables has moved me to pick up a shining pepper or bunch of scarlet radishes just to admire their perfection. I stood by Alice Powers, a beloved local artist, one morning as she did this. Pointing to her basket of eggplant and squash, she said: "They are too beautiful to roast. I want them in a painting."

I learned a lot about flawless peppers and radishes during two seasons as an Assistant Vegetable Gardener. For two of us, our garden was ambitious in size. Rototilled out of a flourishing nursery of immortal weeds, it lay between the house and a woodlands inhabited by herds of deer and other herbivores. Seed packets arrived, spreading across the dining table and into happy conversations on planting. I will forever be cheerful in the presence of a seasonal display of seeds, lifting a packet or two just to read the instructions and feel the hope available for such a small price. Growing vegetables is raised to a spiritual level when we return that small kernel to earth, and with our labor and care, the earth gives back to us. How fitting that the garden should begin on Good Friday … the peas. Sometimes their first moisture came from snow. I do not recall the order in which the rest of our large garden was planted, but I remember the daily discoveries: a line of frothy green over the unseen carrots, small bean tendrils climbing the poles, the blossoms of the cucumber and squash, the scent of dill. One of my last acts of love toward that garden was pulling the large onions, weaving the tops into braided strings and hanging these beautiful garlands of vegetables in the back shed where they lasted far into the winter.

This page from the chronicles was inspired by my weekly trip to the farmers' market. I find the tables of homemade jams and bread, fresh berries and, of course, the vegetables more satisfying than a trip to

Lord & Taylor. At season's end, the tables can only offer the last of the gardens: garlic, potatoes, onions and the ever bountiful zucchini. Customers and vendors at this week's market exchanged recipes for zucchini bread, calling ingredients back and forth. I purchased a squash large enough to try several breads; and also brought home three final tomatoes which still smelled of summer. I'm a happy cowgirl.

UNDERCOVER

Will be undercover. Going "deep" for this operation. Leaving at dawn wearing camouflage jacket and hat. Working silently as possible, I will creep up to the prepared trenches and quickly plant tulips before my squirrels and chipmunks are alerted by the crow intelligence who keep a perimeter close to the back deck. I sneak my bulbs into the ground, covering them in white pepper, black pepper, red pepper, deer/rabbit/mice/raccoon/lost moose repellant. Now you can appreciate my love of tulips, especially the one or two survivors. Perhaps I may find these when this winter ends... a combatant strain of clever tulips blossoming under the birdfeeder.

DUCK EMPIRE

Greetings from Squaw Point Duck Empire on Opening Day. The two Emperors of this shoreline, Jeff and Trent, are out there in a morning fog bank waiting out those tense moments as day (and, hopefully, the fog) breaks. I can just make out two heads above the outline of the blind, so I know they are still high and dry. This year's blind required some engineering to place it above the rising water in the bay. The new platform did not allow for the camo wet suits; however, the two hunters are in hip boots which make the trip to and from the blind a heavy slog. I can imagine the conversation between them and the happy excitement of this morning at the water's edge. Basically, the ducks are not all that important.

ICY ROADS

My vehicle and I traveled all the way to Rapid River before giving up on the trip and heading back to home. Actually, I gave up on other drivers sliding in front of my vehicle on the roadway; and left it to those guys behind me maxing 6 mpg in their monster trucks seeking to acquire a Mighty Honda hood ornament. Since I was driving to my annual medical evaluation in Escanaba, I thought it wise to just return home in my present excellent health rather than have my blood pressure checked as the jaws of life removed me from under a SuperDuty F-450. I write this at fireside, enjoying a cup of Molly's Richmond tea and a precious, seasonal pumpkin donut as MH sheds the first slush and ice of the season onto the garage floor.

JANUARY SPRING CLEANING

I have been regretting my decision to stay at home this winter. These recent weeks find me missing all my friends who have gone south, causing me to think that I was not tolerating the whole winter thing as well as I used to. Then I decided I would get busy and do some "spring" cleaning as long as I was more or less housebound. Washing dust from the log beams, from cupboard tops and baseboards is almost energizing… until the next day. Mature women who have occasional flirtations with asthma should engage in seasonal cleaning during the proper season. Without fresh spring air coming through the windows, the dust I displaced found a new home in my lungs. And so, coughing, chilled, a little lonesome, I promised myself a break next winter. I'm going where my friends are sitting in lawn chairs, having get-togethers on decks, wading in warm water.

My dominoes table is coming over tonight. We will eat leftover Christmas candy and enjoy each other's company, thankful that we are able to be out and about in this weather. Certainly, we will mildly badmouth all those cowards who are fair-weather Yoopers unable to appreciate the beauty of our winter. I will be deceitful during these conversations, and just suck on a cough drop.

PACKER CARDIOLOGY

Being a Packer fan is a sport in itself. Local cardiologists actually have a space on the compulsory Health Summary which requires office patients and emergency room admissions to declare yes/no to being a Packer Backer. Those extra 100 pounds and pack a day will get you a stern reminder from the heart docs, but knowing you will put on the green and gold and watch Packer football places you on their special "watch" list. Viewing Packer games can be like parasailing off Mt. Everest. Exciting, but you don't really want to end up at the bottom, just sorta keep sailing around near the top. Last night my tear-stained Clay Matthews jersey and I were ready to call it a season when Rogers threw the Hail Mary, and cardiologists all over the U.P. began checking their messages. I lay awake into the wee hours, sorting out if I really saw that pass or dreamed it.

ONE-STOP SHOPPER

When the temperature soared to 4 degrees, I decided this was a fine day to drive to town. With all the U.P. elders advising each other to "stay home and stay warm" during the past week's brutal cold, many of us suburbanites around Stonington hunkered down. As expiration dates in the pantry began to fade into the past and milk climbed the food pyramid to one dash a day in the morning coffee, I made my lists and departed the safety of the woods.

A drive to Escanaba, in favorable conditions, is generally 40 minutes. A few tracks of Delbert McClinton's "Nothing Personal" or a little

Bob and Tom in the morning. Poor planning will force you to turn around in Rapid River when the road and adjoining landscape begin to vanish into a whiteout. If you can still see the highway, the slush may slow you down enough to require a short stop in Gladstone (point of no return) to make phone calls changing appointment times. When you decide to continue on without hope of better weather, you must be prepared to think about the trip back home every minute of your time in Escanaba. This gives meaning to the term "one stop shopping" or "as few as possible stops shopping." Drive-thru lunches can be eaten in the parking lot at Elmer's Market. Schedule pedicures only during months without an R in them.

SUBZERO

The third week of January, 2018 behind us, we rise each morning to check the landscape beyond frosted windows, hoping for a break in the icy blasts… just a little blue sky or, at least, a glimpse of the shoreline across the bay. Our county road has been treacherous, grounding even the Mighty Honda, its snow tires frozen to the cement in my unheated garage. Traditionally fearless Lutherans along the Stonington Peninsula, in an unprecedented form of surrender to earthly circumstance, cancelled church. We waited out the weather to the sounds of subzero in the stillness between wind: crunching footsteps along the shoveled path, a startling whoomph from the ice layers on the bay and, at night, beyond the cocoon of the old down quilt, the snap and creak of the house in the cold.

CELEBRATION

Thank you for the world so sweet.
Thank you for the food we eat.
Thank you for the birds that sing.
Thank you, God, for everything.

"A Child's Prayer" Anonymous

PHONE CALLS

Beautiful Barb of Beaufort called this morning as she was packing a small sandwich and her favored fig newtons for another day at the dialysis center. She will repeat this routine twice more this week, hoping for a small renal miracle, but knowing at our age such medical wonders are less and less probable. The conversation shared the happy news of our children and grandchildren, the beginning bloom of the South Carolina piedmont and early spring in the U.P. Crazy Rita is now legally blind, and struggles with new surroundings daily, clearing paths through Baltimore with her cane and threats shouted in Albanian. Our conversation this week was a hilarious mix of the virtues of libertarianism and the best recipe for Spanakopita… and the grandchildren. Nancy called in the evening on Thursday. With the first hours of spring in the Kalamazoo countryside, she is in her gardens, and she had come into the house after a day trimming the raspberry bushes. She did throw in a remark about physical therapy appointments putting her somewhat behind schedule; but she, too, begins and ends these conversations with family news, acknowledging that we are indeed lucky. I do enjoy little phone calls from the kids and local friends I see regularly. We use these opportunities to air our news of car trouble, expired sale coupons, failed recipes, etc. I am convinced that it is healthy to grumble or seek empathy at times. It's just that as my oldest friends and I age and our phone calls to each other become more important to us, I see that we choose to avoid complaining about things we cannot change, and we discuss those we think we can … our kids and grandchildren.

TEA

As politicians in Washington battled and sniped, athletes demeaned our national anthem, great areas of our country were afire or flooded, the city which gave us laughter and dreams lay awash in the filth of its underside … Frances and I sat down to tea. At a table laid with traditional service and her tribute to hydrangeas, we shared our heritage and a favorite subject: books and/or just the words that fill them. Frances is a gifted poet, and I was delighted when she pulled out sheets of notebook paper and read two beautiful, freshly penciled poems inspired by an invitation to tea. She had asked me which variety I liked. Black, fragrant and softened with milk, as my grandmother drank it, taking time for "a cuppa" with a small granddaughter who adored her. Some happy memories you do not mess with. Thank you, Frances, for your friendship and that lovely teapot filled with black tea. Wishing that more people could sit down to moments of civility in a warm and welcoming place to talk of family and beyond …. while enjoying a cup of good tea.

CHEERFUL

I was a cheerful Yooper until a friend in Florida posted a satellite image of Michigan recorded yesterday. There, in varying grades of whiteness, streaked by lines of squalls and jagged with lake effect blizzard, was the scary documentation of winter along the Great Lakes. Miles below outer space, as the wind chill reached minus 40 degrees, I put on the old regulation pea coat, Packers chook, ski gloves and swampers, shoved the door open and went out to clear a path to the garage. It's what Yoopers do. During our winters, when the weather or life in general takes a turn, a little shoveling makes us feel energized. Sadly, it was only January. We had over three weeks before we "broke the back of winter" and could begin rejoicing in precious minutes of increasing sunlight and merciful temperatures. Cozy by my fire later, even as the cold clung to the corners of the rooms, I continued clipping new recipes and reading from the Times "recommended" list as the holiday ham bone simmered in the soup pot. Looking at yesterday's photo, I could only think of frigid desolation and how disappointing this was for the dinosaurs. However, down below on earth, in Michigan, on the Stonington Peninsula, the balsams are always green and fragrant, the irrepressible Yooper birds huddle daily at the feeder and our worst storms leave behind a fresh new landscape. It seems a different world when you fine tune your perception and remain cheerful. Otherwise, it's enough to make you want to go out and shovel.

GREETER

There is an underground society of gracefully aging women who keep secrets… small deceits involving weird recipe substitutions or missing tv remotes and car keys. The cell phone rings on the dining table as you drive past the halfway point into town or sadly beeps inside your car hours after you are safely home. We are those still blessed with memory as age slowly steals it from less fortunate; and we look upon the awareness of these small lapses as, in itself, a Godsend. With confidence in our abilities, we are bonded by a desire to spare loving and watchful children unnecessary and misdirected concern. Small slips are classified information within our society.

Late one afternoon in November, I loaded my groceries into the trunk of Mighty Honda, together with my car keys. As darkness fell over the parking lot, and as in many dark times, I called Auntie Carol. She would drive to my house, pick up an extra key, drive from Stonington to Gladstone, a time frame of roughly an hour. Rush hour at the IGA found me sitting on a box of cider jugs in the entrance, sharing space and time with the Salvation Army bellringer in between visits with roughly a quarter of the population of Delta County. The bellringer claimed I boosted contributions as customers stopped to visit. I sorted and lined up carts a few times and turned in a purse to the Service Desk left in one cart … in recognition of which the management brought a folding chair to me in the entrance. My new friend told me good stories about his regular job far from the red kettle. During the winter months he does volunteer work, but for years of summers he has worked for Skerbeck: operating carnival rides, assembling, tearing down, traveling with them. I now have inside information on the order of setup, maintenance and his thoughts on the escalation of dangerous thrills in amusement parks. The above is not an incident for the "secret" files. It is an event suitable for sharing. Besides, too many people are already telling my family they saw me waiting for rescue.

SWIMMER

As Olympic swimmers thrash the water in Rio, a letter from Beautiful Barbara of Greenville reminded me of another thumbs up for the Soo schools as we knew them. Beginning grade 5, we were trooped over to the high school pool for swim time. Miss Kent and her whistle were at poolside with us regularly for the next 7 years. In that era, we were required to swim one length of the pool to graduate from high school. I doubt they do that sort of thing anymore. Barb and I recalled arriving home on some winter days with our hair frozen where it spilled out of our head coverings. Long pipes punched with holes blew warm air into the locker room, but we didn't always take the time to stand around until our hair dried. And, of course, we walked home in those Spartan days, even when the temperature dropped below zero. Barb now swims in a pool at their retirement community. She is the lone swimmer, churning up the lane, as a gathering of women her age in flowered swim caps grasp the side of the pool in the shallows and jump up and down, pausing to towel the splashes from their faces or to yank on their Roxanne swimwear. You Go Girl!

AFTERTHOUGHT

Dodging the overgrown Easter plants and bins of jellybeans and Peeps, I took a shortcut through the children's section. At the end of one aisle a rack of little girls' purses was being shopped by a small customer. She had slung a purse over her shoulder and was parading back and forth on an imaginary runway. Shiny black patent glittered with circles of silver sparkles… an excellent choice for this year's fashion-wise pre-schooler. A short distance down the aisle, the mother held a cart which carried a fussing baby and a toddler whose patience was also wearing thin. I could see her sorting the packages of small underwear by price. When the little girl approached her mother clutching the purse, I didn't have to hear what she asked; and I already knew what her mother would have to say to her. The purse made one more trip along the magical runway before it was returned to the rack. I wanted so badly to buy that purse as a gift. Let's think for a moment how the mother might feel about that. And looking down the road, that purse might be just the right memory to plant a small seed of motivation. Almost all great achievers had wanted something that wasn't simply given to them. It's a big stretch, I know, from this thought I had in WalMart this morning about achieving because you want a better life for yourself, your family … or even just a shiny, sparkly purse someday. But, this morning, recalling that little girl enjoying something beautiful, I am haunted by my thinking. Sometimes we can follow our hearts … and reasoning be damned. Will I ever stop wishing I had bought that little purse???

HAIRCUT

Every time I make an appointment to have my hair mowed, we get six more weeks of winter. I sometimes admire ladies who have standing appointments at (what I still call) the beauty parlor. Their neat appearance never wavers between regular visits with a hair stylist. I also have friends whose illness has moved hair … or lack of it … far down the list of concerns. As with most groups, I fall solidly in the middle. Therefore, cancelling my haircut this morning was only somewhat disappointing. The latest blast of snow and a rollover at Squaw Creek kept me back in the nest. My Groundhog Day. I am here experimenting with small braids, backcombing and/or hairspray until Weather Underground clears another hair day that won't jinx the season. Hopefully, before I have to change the photo on my driver's license.

PASSWORDS

I am beginning to look my age. This is fine with me, feeling as I do that I have earned each grey hair. I celebrate every laugh line, and can still see a dear face and hear the laughter and stories of friends and family. My vehicle and I are able to head down the road yet, each with only occasional tweaking. But I am acting my age in more and more situations. Recently, I crossed the line into that territory of cranky old ladies who have lost patience with the internet while being submerged in a sea of protocol. I was swept over the edge by a www used to claim "reward" points on a credit card. These had accumulated for some years, reaching a total that offered attractive merchandise, and triggering a fear that this program would discontinue any minute... such as air miles... when you threaten the profit margin. Creating a profile to enter the site took time, spent, mostly, trying to come up with a password. Eventually, within compliance, it looked like this: WhY38*@OmY5926*%#VcpNDHJ)#(!. (Sorry if I used up someone's future choice) Security questions (3) were tricky, suggesting the name of great grandma's first boyfriend, model number of first car I drove, etc. I eventually broke through to the website which allowed me a look at their catalog, showing that the only item I wanted was discontinued.

I am purging the kitchen drawer full of notebooks and journals in which I have stored such secret information traded with websites for small attentions. I am hanging up on any service providers who won't come up with a live representative within two buttons on my phone. When a recorded voice says: "Your business is important to us...", I don't believe them. I am now down to three passwords, a manageable amount of secrecy for someone of my years who, occasionally, forgets where her present car is parked, much less the name of the first vehicle she drove.

DREGS

Winter has been kinder to us. The monotony of the temperature is confirmed by the resolute levelness from the edge of my woods to the treeline across the bay. I should say: "so far, so good." No towering whitecaps of U.P. powder curling toward the roofline, burying power lines along the peninsula and boosting sales of trucks with second stories. A good polar vortex gets Yoopers, such as myself, perking. You won't find this in your holistic manual, but if winter seems to drag on, change the environment. (By now my pc is lighting up with all sorts of mail from Al Gore.) I change the furniture around, move the fairy lights from the Boston fern to the Christmas cactus, finally frame the graduation photos, Class of '51. Today I am enjoying the most pleasurable result of my recent mid-winter therapy. In the kitchen, paperwhite bulbs have found new life in Po's amberglass dish as the leavings of the winter arrangement, still beautiful with stems of money plant, wild cranberry and gilded birch twigs, keep their place on the old cocktail table. I am in the environment I love, and need only to walk a few steps to change the season. But, oh, to open the windows and smell the mock orange some day!

MILES TO GO

Thanks Ryan Beggs for sharing those cheerful ads telling me dealers are practically giving away Happy Hondas for Christmas. My Honda is not so Happy right now as it awaits major surgery at Jerry's Service Ctr; but, at 170,000 miles, it has earned a little tender care. The two of us have many miles to go yet together. So, Honda, you can keep your sweet smelling, fully loaded and shiny new models. My dependable wheels and I trust each other like good friends; and if we each smell a little like French fries and have a few wrinkles and scrapes, we both have heart ... and everyone knows it's what's under the hood that counts.

RECONCILIATION

A few hours before our 55th class reunion, July, 2006, my dear friend Rita Perroy and I had words. We did not speak to each other for 9 years, 21 days, 10 hours. Careless words, tossed off in an angry moment. Only six words gathered up our happiest years together: dances, boyfriends, marriages, children, divorces, wild and crazy weekends, times of consolation and support to each other... threw them all into a dark corner to be unmentioned, disregarded. Yesterday afternoon I answered the phone to be greeted by: "Hi... it's a voice from the past." My friend, Crazy Rita, is now living in Baltimore, in a retirement situation, near her son, Peter, and his family. She has advanced macular degeneration, but ventures to nearby shops with a cane and her fierce spirit. She "reads" voraciously, as always, with the help of a tape player and recorded books. She still comments forcefully on televised sports broadcasts and, of course, politics. The fashionable Rita is able to coordinate her wardrobe with visual aids to sort out colors. We talked for two hours. No apologies were necessary, no tears ... just us again. Paul said, **"Let no corrupting talk come out of your mouths, but only such as is good for building up, as fits the occasion, that it may give grace to those who hear."** (Ephesians 4:29)

FIRST KISS

The story of my friendship with Donald always includes the part about how we practiced kissing each other; and when he became really good at it, he asked Barbara Prohazka (now Larsen, "Beautiful Burba of Beaufort") to go steady with him. But few people knew about the first kiss. We were 8 years old when our parents took a trip to Wisconsin together, which included children. Donald and I were sent to cot beds in the porch, and we told each other stories until we were sleepy, and then he just came over to my cot, said good night, and kissed me on my cheek. It is the Donald I remember... tender, caring, the kind of male friend every girl should have. And fun. We both loved to swim and spent our summers in the waters of Bay Mills and Monocle Lake, competing in underwater distance, speed and small moments of daring when we stripped off our bathing suits behind one of the boats moored offshore. That ended when we, sadly, became modest. I was his first passenger the day he picked up his driver's license. He needed a little extra cash for some gas and stopped by for me and my fortune of a few bucks. Our parents tracked us down about the same time the gas ran out. His obituary says a lot about Donald after 1951; and I know he brought much happiness to other lives. We didn't get to share any of those years; therefore, I am left with this beautiful thought of him swimming underwater at Monocle Lake...

PRAYERFUL

Driving down the peninsula to our little church in the wilderness on Sunday mornings is a prayerful experience. The winter months challenge even my trusted snow tires as they struggle for traction on the ice, piloted through whiteouts by an ancient but fearless driver. But on the first Summery Sunday such as yesterday, the road to Trinity inspires more joyful prayer. The wildest pin cherry trees now blossom delicately throughout the woods. Trillium and marsh marigold flourish among the fiddle fern shoots as deer graze comfortably on the bounty to the very edge of their wildwood garden.

OPEN WATER

Temperatures soar to above freezing. A pair of Canada geese have booked into my shoreline for the season, and appear to be once again scouting the marshy edge of my neighbors' boardwalk. The Clowers family labored during months of good weather to complete this project last year only to be bullied for weeks by the nesting geese settled in next to the walkway. The sand hill cranes have made it through another winter, returning to my beach to nest and eventually delight me with two or three of nature's ugliest offspring. They will court in my front yard, sharing this annual honeymoon with me as if I am a guest at the wedding and, I like to think, in appreciation of remembered safety and friendship.

CYBER INTERVENTION

Hello Facebook friends... I did miss you, and have been filling up that cyber void created by my laptop's total withdrawal. The "Cooking Light" recipe clippings have been sorted by calorie count. Mysteries have been solved as I invaded closets and bottom drawers. Nephew DJ, who specializes in Emergency Electronic Interventions, to the rescue. Rehabilitation (still talking about the laptop here) has been successful if you are reading this. And then my cell phone staged a protest, allowing me to send and receive, but refusing to display calls or alerts on the screen. I imagined the voicemail lady sounding a tad grumpy with me for relying on her to constantly recite missed calls. Calling out was risky without the numbers on the screen. NOTE TO SELF: Remove Johnny Depp from speed dial. He didn't believe I was really trying to call my chiropractor.

CHANGEOVER

This is sorta the Monday of changeover. The last of the visiting cousins have departed their places out here and headed back to Colorado, Minnesota, the Carolinas, etc. We permanent family are left to return the empties, distribute the leftover bratwurst buns and check the windows and doors of cottages one more time. The Monday Morning Quilters are back on task, in earnest, this morning... only eight weeks until hunting season and its raffle opportunities. I see my neighbors pulling their docks, dodging the hollow protests of the feathered squatters who will soon be flying South from Squaw Point. The driftwood bonfires of summer nights are happy daydreams, and before long we will stand over an afternoon burn of leaves and the final garden trimmings, thinking of how we will revive the beach and empty bedrooms next summer. Our family will have a new little face around the fire then; and the small water shoes lined up in the beach shed will be reshuffled and waiting.

WHISKER RUB

This First Day of Deer Season brings a memory of Daddy coming home from camp with a beard and his three little girls waiting for a "whisker rub," hugging the big man as if he had returned from months in outer space. We buried our faces in the old Soo Woolen Mills shirt and its distinctive camp bouquet: woodsmoke, fried bacon, cigars... and something elusive which may have been satisfying beer farts. Later, the result of the happiest time of the year for hunters would materialize on the stove, frying in a pan with onions, as the hunter recalled the day and place he saw the big buck, and sparing his family the details of how it got from the Naomikong to our kitchen. That was when we all loved venison ... or said we did because we loved the hunter. Awesome steps to follow, boys ... into the woods.

JEFFREY

Here we are celebrating your buck. Hunting Camp is such a tradition in our family, isn't it. I can still remember the smell of my dad›s hunting shirt when he came home and he always had to give us cheek rubs with his beard ... little girls running around screaming and loving it. My mother shying away and claiming he smelled like mice poop, but happy just seeing him. It seemed as if every guy was called by a nickname at camp: Butch (Dad), Mush (Larsen), Mick (McKee) that I remember.

First names were too **everyday** for such a sacred place. Your Grampa
Ed is smiling because you get to enjoy so many of the happy times he
had. And I've been sitting here thinking how to assure you that though
some of those days are past (not gone), how wonderful to have lived
them and to have the memories. And each new hunting season ... each
new day (if I want to get really preachy)... is going to be a wonderful
memory someday that we will enjoy reliving. I liked you recalling the
cigars and three bean salad: small things which perfect a memory. I
will remember you telling me these thoughts, sitting here the two of
us, on a sunny morning, while the bay is fighting off the beginning ice
and a few mallards have shown up for the occasion. It is my new good
memory, Jeff.

THANKSGIVING

Our family celebrates Thanksgiving the old fashioned way, gathering
together as many of us as possible in the same city, at the same house, at
the same time. My earliest Thanksgiving memories go back to the "big
table" at the Sawyers farm seating grandparents, aunts, uncles, cousins ...
the entire family. Faithful Presbyterians, my grandparents were first
generation "settlers" in the Pickford farm area; my parents and their
siblings were survivors of the recent Great Depression. We were blessed
with the important things: family and faith and a shared bountiful
meal. The secret to a fine dressing is still a topic of conversation as
it was back when Nanny Sawyers was in charge. This generation has
been spared Aunt Reta's suet pudding, but her recipe is preserved on a
sticky card in my mother's cookbook. The day was spent visiting and
preparing, but the meal was enjoyed and cleared before milking time;
and we all drove off down the Old Pickford Road for home. Some of us
had nearly 20 miles to travel. In Houghton, Escanaba, the Naomikong,
North Dakota, North and South Carolina, Colorado, Florida, the
family will observe Thanksgiving at new tables. The faces and settings
change, but the blessings of family and faith celebrated at a bountiful
table have been handed down ... and we are thankful all.

LEFTOVERS

The kids delivered their leftover turkey today, bearing it to my kitchen on the ceremonial old pan like some religious artifact. I am always thankful for this post-holiday tradition of making, as they call it, turkey carcass soup. Two big soup kettles are simmering on the stove, filled with the first rough leftovers, which will be strained and sorted, leaving that wonderful broth cooking with onion, celery and first of the seasonings. Meanwhile, I am cleaning the refrigerator of elderly vegetables: carrots, a part of a cabbage, a serving of spinach, a dish of peas ...whatever. I may sneak in a few spoonsful of leftover rutabagas or cauliflower if they are hanging around on the lower shelf. All good stuff. It goes into the pots to cook away for the rest of the afternoon, filling my house with that wonderful "soup's on" smell. Eventually, one pot gets rice, the other, pasta; and as I fill the freezer containers for the family and myself, the vegetable peels will be providing a special treat for my little woodland neighbors. Turkey carcass, the gift that keeps on giving.

TREASURE

Yearly, one of the boys stops by to hand down the boxes filled with Christmas stored under the eaves. Kim is catching up on some family times celebrated while she was living in Colorado; and last week she was at the top of the ladder reaching for pieces of her childhood and the Christmases she missed during recent years. We had a memorable afternoon opening the boxes and sharing stories unwrapped and enjoyed like the treasure we sorted through. Last year it was Tom's turn to hand down Christmas, as shared in anniecat's story......

"Tommy has been in Stonington the past few days closing up his cabin for the winter. He took a drive down my road for coffee, and found himself atop a ladder handing down Christmas. Each year I am surprised at the amount of treasure hidden under the eaves waiting to be reclaimed. Do stored decorations multiply in the dark like items in that special kitchen drawer which always needs a good cleaning? As each box comes down, we note the message I have printed on it in large letters. On the top of the heap is the small MANGER box holding the F.W. Woolworth nativity my dad brought home for his daughters. Following, in order of breakability the cartons appear: the BASKET from Scott, my mother's treasured WISE MEN (who really did travel from the East because they came from the mantel in our home at the Soo to my mantel in the Stonington cottage), the TREE DECORATIONS which take up three boxes, the FRYKEN figures for the lighted shelf over the dining table, and the WRAPPING box which should come out first because each year I vow to wrap gifts right away. Tom and I recite the boxes as they come down the ladder, filled with memories of those happy Christmases Past, and bringing with them that joyful "Christmas Is Coming" feeling to my child, Tommy, and me."

What a treasure for her mother is a daughter. Especially if, as with my daughter, Kim, you are of one heart. We share the love and responsibility for her brothers and their families, as well as the joy of each other's company in quiet moments ... and the pure happiness of simple fun that comes with having the same reckless spirit. I love and admire Kim endlessly for her thoughtfulness to others, her courage and strength, and for being my dearest friend forever.

Her brothers brought me three women I cherish like daughters and enjoy as fun and trusted friends: Cherie, Laurie and Pam. They in turn have brought us the beloved grandchildren: Ryan, Amy, Kellee, Abby and Molly... and those angels who are a special blessing of a long, happy life, the greatgrands: Henrik, Axel, Sawyer, Beau, Lance, Skylar and Jakob.

CELEBRATION

As my friend JC would remind me, I have now begun my next trip around the sun, having completed 84 outrageously wonderful rides. I've had great company, having been joined along the way by my children who give my life purpose and great happiness. I know the joy and pride that grandchildren bring; I now have a great-granddaughter I am looking forward to meeting and have held my great-grandsons, watching them with a touch of sadness, knowing how far they will reach beyond me. Looking at my messages from my family and my friends, I am reminded it is wonderful to have them all to share the journey when it is bumpy, and to celebrate the smooth sailing. These years are a gift, their worth more appreciated when we realize God didn't intend for us to waste them. My birthday began in church to reassure Him I am mindful of this, but after the visits with family that I love, I ended the day watching "Pink Panther"... He expects us to keep being a little crazy and enjoying the ride.

MOMENTS

Sharing hard times with someone can bring comfort and sometimes new insight; but, always keep the happy times on the top shelf where they are easily relived with others, bringing pleasure to them in the sharing.

Anniecat Chronicles

Scarlet Tanager. My first encounter. He perched just above me in the tree under which I was resting. We were companionable for some time. Eventually, he lost interest in this tree (and me) and moved from branch to branch in surrounding trees. I wished for two things as I watched him: (1) that there would be a nest on my property someday and (2) that I had a camera with me. My bird book describes this little bird as "blindingly beautiful" and notes they like oak trees. If we become neighbors, we already have something in common ...

The youngest wild child, Scott, arrives today from Florida to celebrate his birthday with Mom (and Tom, Jeff, Kim, Cuz Deej, Auntie Carol, et al.). We will bundle him in warm clothes and ancient boots, feed him family favorite meals let him wander into the woods with his brothers. From the Cayman Islands, Key West, Ft. Lauderdale, to the "retirement ranch" near Ocala, it's a rare winter visit from this dear man who can't outgrow being "little brother" ...

Just as I throw the last shovelful off my drifted walkways and begin my "cool down" stride back to the house, the skies open and deliver the promised "deteriorating weather conditions." By the time I reach the back door, Gladstone has disappeared from sight across the bay. The thing about being a conscientious shoveler is deciding which requires less effort ... clearing the snow once a day or waiting out bad weather and dealing with larger accumulations. Such things to ponder keep me from worrying about Washington ... which, by the way, could use a lot of shoveling out ...

Tom was in Stonington this weekend checking on his cabin down the road from me. Late yesterday as he settled in for a night in the winter woods the unmistakable howl came from the trees just behind his garage. Tom is not given to drama, but described the sound as chilling, unforgettable. His mother's imagination has stayed with the wolf all day. Was he warning off the intruder or merely making his presence known. Perhaps in the frozen isolation of a February night a wolf was moved to cry out to someone familiar...

A lovely photo of a gardenia popped up on my fb page while the steady wintry drizzle turned to snow again. Hollyhocks are my favorite, but I admire gardenias. And they go to proms with you... pinned in a corsage or nestled just behind an ear. A gardenia says *elegant*. Its exotic scent does not suit just anyone. Short-lived, all its beauty is brought to that one, special evening, refusing, afterwards, to live in a glass of tap water...

I remember being in Sault Ste. Marie on the date the Fitzgerald sank near Whitefish. We had a radio on, listening for up to minute news. Terrible sadness in a town where streets began and ended on a great shipping lane, and everyone waved to the men on deck as they cleared the locks. Our Jeff sailed on the Middleton for two years, and I remember walking along the fence to speak to him for a few minutes as his ship locked through. On foggy nights we heard the ships calling to each other as we drifted, safely, off to sleep. There was courage aboard the Fitzgerald that night, and her crew earned their rest below the storm...

This morning I have two young does peeking at me through the railing of the front deck. The winter has been hard on them. The veggie peels I toss out the door daily for "first come, first served" in my animal kingdom have been a treat for them, and they are cautiously curious about my movements in the kitchen. I know... in a few weeks they will move on to nibble at my budding hydrangeas and the carefully planted spring blooms. But, these two survivors are surely carrying new life in their starved bodies. They wait politely, fixing those soft eyes on me and the two fresh apples I carry to the sliding glass door...

I opened my private messages last evening to a little line from Emily "no video, just audio!" And a brief click brought me one of my life's most beautiful gifts. I heard Emily singing whispery soft and a small voice following her in an unforgettable duet of "Silent Night." Sawyer Daniel, 23 months, is too young to realize the radiance of such a moment... he surely won't remember it. But I carry it with me in my heart, Sawyer, where you are always with me....

Sunday morning Pastor Diane sat on the floor with the children, as is her custom for the children's sermon. With the altar behind her and nestled beside two little girls, the sermon went well; but, when the children were dismissed to scamper back to their parents, Pastor Diane was left tied to the altar by the cinctures on her vestment. Small fingers, unnoticed, had quietly created a project with the interesting cords. We have brought our praise, grief, disappointment, fear and hope to Jesus during Sunday services. How wonderful to give Him a good laugh…

The trees have been holding on to summer and fall through these unusually warm days. This morning a drizzle of cold rain is mixed with a steady shower of falling leaves. It is as if, like us, the trees have breathed a great sigh and given up to the arrival of winter…

These stories are for:

MOONBIZ C. Thompson (Tom) Beggs Gave himself the name MoonBiz so I would stop calling him Tommy Tiddlemouse. His mother's first guardian and little fixit child. The patient one with a gift for engines, a love of his family, fast boats, hi-fi and the rock it produces. He is a born performer with a sharp wit to keep us all from taking each other seriously.

MUGGINS Jeffrey Edward Beggs The remake of his Grampa Ed, he is the loving watchdog of our family; the wild young adventurer turned devoted husband, father and Papa Jeff. The tattoos, vintage Harley, hunting and fishing all take a back seat to FaceTime, storybooks and this family's needs. His wisdom, sense of humor and honesty have saved us all.

PEANUT (PIGLET in earlier days while her brothers' brains were still undeveloped) Kimberly Sue Beggs The only daughter, she became her brothers' fiercest defender and the family conscience and heart as well as her mother's joy and sidekick. All strength, creativity, fun, energy, thoughtfulness and love in a beautiful package.

BUMBIE Scott Calvin Beggs. That would be the child so sweet he was called "Bumbie" ... baby mispronounced ... who became a commanding 6'2" man. Our Favorite Uncle, world traveler, businessman, former executive chef and, recently, part-time Florida chicken farmer. But even if he outgrew the name, he will never lose the enchanting lovability which inspired it.

Thank you, once again to BFF Darlene N. Prokos, gifted artist and dear friend, for capturing the spirit of this little book in her beautiful cover.

And if you are reading all this, join me in thanking my nephew Dan Beggs (Cousin Deej) for helping, as always, to rescue my words from electronic evaporation.